P9-CQW-647

ROTTEN SCHOOL series:

ROTTEN SCHOOL

GROWTH LEARNING PIZZA!

CALLING ALL BIRDBRAINS

R.L. STINE

Illustrations by Trip Park

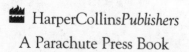

HarperCollins*Publishers*

A Parachute Press Book

For Lawson
–TP

Calling All Birdbrains
Copyright © 2007 by Parachute Publishing, L.L.C.
Cover copyright © 2007 by Parachute Publishing, L.L.C.

All rights reserved.
No part of this book may be used or reproduced in any manner whatsoever without written permission except in the case of brief quotations embodied in critical articles and reviews. Printed in the United States of America.
For information address HarperCollins Children's Books, a division of HarperCollins Publishers, 1350 Avenue of the Americas, New York, NY 10019.
www.harpercollinschildrens.com

Library of Congress Cataloging-in-Publication Data is available.
ISBN 978-0-06-123275-6 (trade bdg.) — ISBN 978-0-06-123276-3 (lib. bdg.)

Cover and interior design by mjcdesign
09 10 11 12 13 CG/RRDB 10 9 8

First Edition

—:CONTENTS:—

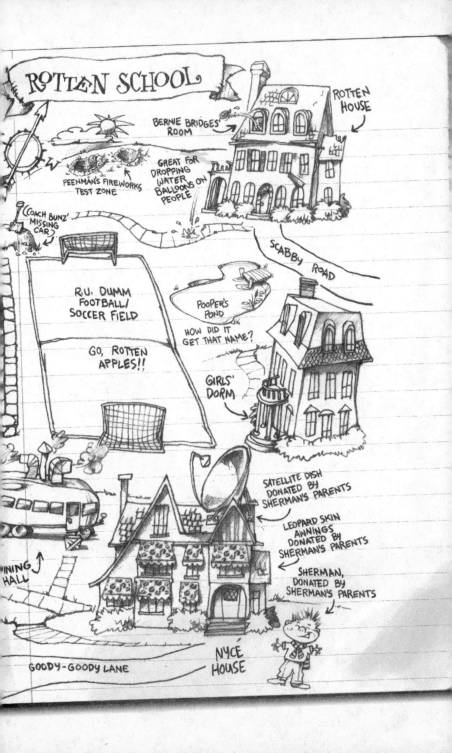

MORNING ANNOUNCEMENTS

Good morning, Rotten Students. This is Headmaster Upchuck. Please put away all sharp objects. You know you can't be trusted with sharp objects.

I hope you are all having a Rotten Day. Here are this morning's important announcements....

I'm sorry to announce that third grader Harry Legg is the first student in school history to *flunk* Morning Announcements. I'm sure Harry will do much better when he repeats third grade next year.

Chef Baloney would like all students to know that the object found in the salad last night was *not* a human finger. It was a chimpanzee finger.

Fifth grader Chasen Flyballz will be showing off his pierced tongue at table six in the Dining Hall at lunch. As usual, Chasen will be sitting alone.

The sixth grade Dress-Up Dance will be held tonight in the gym. The theme of the dance is: "Party Till You're Sick." Everyone should come dressed as your favorite disease.

The After-School Big Eaters Club is holding its Charity Burp-Off in the Dining Hall at lunch. The club hopes to raise five hundred dollars for kids in other countries who cannot burp.

Chapter 1

"BITE MY BEAK!"

"Uno!" I cried. I slapped my cards down on the table. "Pay up, guys. Pay up."

Sherman Oaks, that spoiled, rich brat, pulled some money from his gold money clip. He shook his head. "You've won every game, Bernie. I'm down to my last five hundred dollars!"

"When you're hot, you're hot," I said, taking his money. "Come on, total up your cards, Feenman. You owe me big-time!"

Across the table, my friend Crench groaned. "Bernie, you're *unbelievable*. How can one person win TWENTY Uno games in a row?"

I flashed him my million-dollar grin. "Guess I'm just lucky!" I reached up to my shoulder and petted Lippy, my adorable parrot.

"AWWWK. BEAK ME! BITE MY BEAK! I'LL PLUCK YOUR EYES!"

he squawked.

He's so sweet! Who taught him to say those cute things?

He dug his claws into my shoulder as I tickled his feathers. That adorable parrot always warms my heart.

Across the card table, Sherman's pal Wes Updood was still counting his cards. "Do all worms come from Ohio?" he muttered. "Even Gummi Worms? That's just totally Toledo—know what I mean?"

Wes is the coolest dude at Rotten School. He's so totally cool, no one can understand a word he says!

"Goat's milk," Wes muttered. "What's up with goats, anyway? Do they have to be so short? That's totally Toledo. Yo!" He went back to counting his Uno cards.

Feenman yawned so hard, he fell off his chair. He sat on the floor and rubbed his red eyes. "Bernie, what time is it?"

Sherman raised his *huge* gold watch. The watch has so many jewels and so many gadgets, it weighs nearly forty pounds. Sherman usually pays a first grader to carry it around for him.

"Whoa," he said, squinting at the flashing dial. "You wouldn't *believe* the temperature on Mars!"

"I just want to know the time," Feenman said, curling up on the floor.

"It's six in the morning," I said. I pointed to the clock on the wall.

"TIME TO PLUCK YOUR NOSE!"

Lippy chirped. He dug his claws deeper into my shoulder.

Wes and Sherman stood up, shaking their heads, watching me count my winnings. "See you, guys," Sherman said, starting to the door.

"Rather *be* you than *see* you," Wes said.

Did *that* make any sense?

You probably go home after school every day. But

our school is a boarding school. That means we *live* here. We can do whatever we want. No parents! And *that* means staying up all night!

We have our all-night Uno tournaments in a tiny back room in the Student Center. All the lights are out in the building. No one knows we are here.

When we sneak back to our dorms, we have to be very careful. I don't know why—but for some reason, Headmaster Upchuck doesn't approve of all-night card games.

Sherman and Wes closed the door behind them.

Crench jumped to his feet. "Bernie, tell me your secret," he said. "How did you win every game? Tell me! *How?*" He grabbed the front of my shirt—and knocked Lippy off my shoulder.

"AWWWWWWWK!"

The bird let out a cry as he hit the floor. Then he was silent.

"OH NO!"

I gasped. I spun away from Crench and dropped to

the floor in a panic. I scooped up the parrot in my hands. "Lippy, speak to me!" I cried. "*Speak* to me!"

"MAKE MY DAY! CHOKE ON A CUTTLEBONE!"

Lippy squawked.

I cradled Lippy against my chest. "Thank *goodness* you're okay."

Feenman squinted at me. "Bernie, why do you bring that squawking bird to all our card games?" he asked.

"Yeah, he's just a stupid bird. What's the big deal?" Crench said.

My two best buddies in the world, and they didn't understand.

"Hel-lo!" I said. "Just a stupid bird? I don't *think* so! Want to know how I win every game? You're *looking* at him! It's Lippy. He's a *lucky* bird!"

Chapter 2

A NOISY TUG-OF-WAR

I felt something warm and sticky plop into my hand. If only parrots could be housebroken!

"Lippy is a good-luck charm," I explained, wiping my hand off on Crench's jeans. "I can't win without him."

Feenman blinked. "You're joking, right?"

"No joke," I said, tickling Lippy's back. "Haven't you dudes noticed? Every time I bring Lippy to a game, I win big-time."

Feenman and Crench laughed. "Yeah. That bird really knows his cards," Feenman said. "Maybe we should let him deal!"

They both laughed some more.

"Go ahead and make fun," I said. "But this parrot is totally lucky. And not just for card games. Every time he's with me, he brings me good luck."

"AWWWWWK."

Lippy squawked and dropped a huge glob of green bird plop on the floor.

Feenman and Crench jumped away from it. "Bombs away!" Feenman cried.

"How lucky is *that?*" Crench said. "Bernie, get serious. That fat parrot is totally gross."

"Oh, yeah?" I said. "You guys think you're so smart? Look what Lippy was trying to show me."

I pointed to the floor. Next to the glob of bird plop was a dollar bill.

I picked it up and shoved it into my pocket. "See?" I said. "Someone dropped that money. And why did I find it? Because of Lucky Lippy!"

That made them both stop laughing. They stared at Lippy.

"No joke? That loudmouth pile of feathers is

lucky?" Feenman said. "Hey—let me touch him. I want some luck to rub off on me!"

"Yo! Me too!" Crench cried.

They both pounced on Lippy at the same time. Feenman grabbed him around the neck. Crench grabbed the claws.

"Let go!"

Crench shouted.

"You let go!"

Feenman shouted back.

"No, you let go!"

It was an ugly tug-of-war. Feathers flew everywhere. They stretched Lippy out until he was about six feet long!

"Both of you—let go of him!" I cried.

"AWWWWWK!"

the parrot squawked.

"I'LL PECK YOU TILL YOU TWEET!"

"Stop it!"

I screamed. "Are you both *nuts?*" I grabbed my adorable pet back and hugged him to my chest. "Look what you *did* to him!"

Chapter 3

TOTALLY BUSTED

"AWWWWWK! I'LL PECK YOU TILL TUESDAY!"

I held up the poor parrot and examined him. Lippy had a big BALD SPOT on the back of his head.

"Look what you did! You SCALPED him!" I cried.

They both backed away. "We just rubbed him a little. You know. For luck," Crench said.

"AWWWWWK! I'LL PLUCK YOUR NOSE HAIRS!"

I patted Lippy gently. "There, there," I whispered. I had to chuckle. With that bald head, Lippy looked a *lot* like Headmaster Upchuck.

I turned back to my two buddies. "Just keep your paws off my lucky bird," I said.

"No problem," Feenman said, yawning. "See you back at the dorm, Big B." They both shuffled out the door.

I held Lippy gently and tried to smooth his feathers. The poor guy didn't even realize he was bald now.

I set him carefully on my shoulder. Then I crept out the back door of the Student Center.

The morning sun was just coming up. A ribbon of red crossed the sky. The grass was still wet and shiny from the previous night's dew.

I couldn't wait to get back to my room in Rotten House and count my Uno winnings. Walking in the shade under the apple trees, I began trotting over the Great Lawn.

I was halfway across campus when I heard a chilling sound. A man's voice calling me.

"Bernie!"

"Stop right there!"

I froze. Lippy froze, too.

I turned to see Mr. Skruloose running toward me. Mr. Skruloose is the Assistant Headmaster, and he's probably the toughest man on earth. He calls us all "soldier" and acts like we're at war.

Every morning at dawn, he goes on a ten-mile hike. Just for fun.

I took a deep breath as I watched Mr. Skruloose march toward me. Was I busted? Would Skruloose realize I'd been up all night?

He stopped about two inches in front of me. Sweat poured down his forehead. His big muscles rippled under the tight sleeves of his T-shirt.

"Soldier!"

he boomed. "Why are you up at six? And why do you have a parrot on your shoulder?"

He slowly lowered his face to mine. "You'd better have a good answer, Bridges."

Chapter 4

WHO'S A DUMB TWEET?

Was I worried? Nervous? Totally in a panic?

No way.

I knew I could talk my way out of this jam—with my lucky bird there. Lucky Lippy never lets me down.

Mr. Skruloose leaned over me. We were nearly forehead to forehead. I couldn't believe it. The dude had big muscles in his *forehead*!

"Let's hear it, soldier!" he boomed.

I cleared my throat. "Well, sir," I started, "I'm president of the Wildlife Club. Early morning is the best time to wake up and see wildlife stuff—don't you agree?"

He stared at me, trying to decide if I was lying.

"I love to get up before the sun," I said. "If it means I can see exciting wildlife—like this wild African parrot."

Skruloose eyed the parrot.

I stuck out my hand. "Perhaps you'd like to make a donation to the Wildlife Club, sir?" I said. "If you have a spare ten-dollar bill, I know everyone in our club will appreciate it."

I waited for Skruloose to pull out his wallet. He *had* to believe my story. The lucky parrot always brings me luck when I'm in a jam.

"A donation?" Skruloose cried. "Bridges, why should I give you money when you have a big wad of dollar bills in your shirt pocket?"

"Well, I can explain that, sir," I said. "We members of the club need money to protect endangered animals, sir. Like this poor parrot. He—"

"There IS no Wildlife Club!" Skruloose thundered. "You were up all night playing cards—weren't you?"

"No way!" I cried. "Well…maybe…"

Skruloose grabbed my shoulder and lifted me about two feet off the ground. "I'm taking you to Headmaster Upchuck's office," he said. "You can tell him about your all-night card game."

"Huh?"

That's all I could say. I was too dazed to talk.

How could this happen to me, the Great Bernie B.?

I had failed to talk my way out of a jam. That *never* happens—not when I have Lippy with me.

"AWWWK. YOU'RE A DUMB TWEET!"

Lippy called to Skruloose.

"YOU'RE A DUMB TWEET!"

"Think that's funny, Bridges?" Skruloose sneered. "Think I don't know that's *you* imitating a parrot?"

"But, sir—" I started.

"When you're finished with the Headmaster," Skruloose boomed, "come see *me*. We can talk about what's funny and what isn't."

"BIRDBRAIN! BIRDBRAIN!"

Lippy squawked.

Mr. Skruloose's face turned bright red. I think that meant he was kinda angry.

I shook my head as he carried me to the Headmaster's office.

What just happened here? Did Lucky Lippy just get me into even *worse* trouble?

Chapter 5

THE ECCH NEEDS A PARTNER

Headmaster Upchuck lectured me for two hours. He said if he caught me playing cards again, he'd give me an even *longer* lecture.

I said, "Don't worry, sir. You won't catch me."

"Bernie, before you go, here's a bit of advice," Upchuck said. "Whatever it is you *like* to do...don't do it."

"Good advice, sir," I said. I gave him a sharp, two-fingered salute.

"AWWWWK. YOU BALD-HEADED TWEET!"

I gritted my teeth. Was Lippy going to get me into even *more* trouble?

The Upchuck laughed. "Very funny parrot, Bernie," he said. Then his smile faded. "Get rid of him. Pets aren't allowed on campus."

"Pet, sir?" I said. "This bird isn't a pet. He's a wild bird. He migrated here from the west coast of Africa."

Upchuck stared at Lippy. "He flew ten thousand miles and just happened to land on your shoulder?"

"Go figure, sir."

The Headmaster frowned. "Bernie, let me give you one more piece of advice."

"Yes, sir," I said.

"Get out of here!"

Upchuck said.

"Good advice, sir," I said again.

"AWWWWK. EAT BIRD PELLETS!"

I held on to Lippy, turned, and ran out of the Headmaster's office. The morning sun was shining above the trees now, and the air was warm. A beautiful day—but I didn't care.

"Lippy, what's up with you?" I asked. "You didn't help me at all."

The bird leaned down and nipped my earlobe.

"OWWWW!

That really hurts."

I heard the thunder of hoofbeats. The ground shook. It sounded like a cattle stampede.

I looked up—and saw Jennifer Ecch rumbling toward me. Jennifer is big and strong and hulky and tough. She once arm-wrestled a *tree* and WON!

And did I mention that she's totally in love with me?

Do you know how yucky it is to be in fourth grade and have a girl call you "Honey Face" and "Sugar Toes"?

I knew what The Ecch wanted.

She wanted me to be her partner at the annual I. B. Rotten Outdoor Game Competition. The games are a really big deal. They were started by the founder of our school, I. B. Rotten.

The whole school competes. Everyone has to have a partner. They take us in school buses to Lake Choking Gas, where the games are held.

I watched Jennifer bounce over the grass. I knew I had no choice. I had to hide.

No way I wanted to be her partner.

I dove behind a clump of leafy bushes.

Then I dropped to the ground and lay flat in a pile of dead leaves.

Frantically, I began scooping the large, brown leaves over me. In seconds, I was totally buried beneath them.

I held Lippy to my chest and rubbed him for good luck.

"Don't let her find me....Don't let her find me."

Chapter 6

TIME TO START GACKING

A few seconds later, the leaves crackled. Strong hands swept my cover away.

I opened my eyes to see Jennifer Ecch's one blue eye and one brown eye staring down at me. She grabbed me around the waist and picked me up like I was her Barbie doll.

"Good morning, Angel Nose," she boomed. "Are you doing a little nature study down there?"

"Put me down," I said. "And please—don't call me Angel Nose."

She licked my ears for five or ten minutes. Then

she said, "Honey Face, will you be my partner at the I. B. Rotten Games?"

"Huh?" That was my best reply. I was in total shock.

I stared at Lippy. The bird let me down *again*!

What was up with Lucky Lippy?

"TWICK OR TWEET! TWICK OR TWEET!"

he squawked.

"Just shut up," I muttered, clamping my fingers around his beak.

Did the bird's luck run out? Could it happen?

Did my buddies Feenman and Crench *ruin* Lippy when they rubbed him bald? Did they rub away all the good luck?

No way. No way. No way.

I had to give the bird one more try. One more chance to bring Bernie B. some luck ...

"Uh ... Jen, I'm sorry," I said. "But I can't be your partner. I'm in the Club."

She blinked. "What club?"

"You know," I said. "The Club. Very sorry. But you know how it is. The Club comes first."

"Oh, yeah?" Jennifer replied. She grabbed my arm and started to bend it up behind my back.

CRAAAAAAACK.

"You snapped my arm!" I cried. "You SNAPPED it!"

"Honey Breath, I guess that means you're *out of the Club* now," Jennifer said. She had a big, drooly grin on her face. "So now you can be my partner at the Competition."

"Gaaaaack."

I staggered away, holding my arm gently, very gently.

I stumbled toward the dorm, *gaaaack*ing all the way.

Jennifer didn't buy my Club story for a second. I could tell by the way she snapped my arm.

Is Lucky Lippy *Bad-Luck* Lippy now? I wondered.

I pulled the bird off my shoulder and held him in front of me. "Lippy, tell me you're still lucky.

Please—show me. Show me you're still my good-luck charm."

"URRRRRRRP."

The bird burped up something green and pasty onto my shirt.

I turned and saw April-May June jogging over the grass. April-May is the coolest, hottest girl at Rotten School. She's my girlfriend, only she doesn't know it yet.

"April-May! Wait up!" I shouted.

She's so shy. She started to run faster.

"Wait up!" I shouted. I set Lippy on my shoulder and started to run.

"WHOOOOA!" I let out a cry as I tripped over something.

A garden rake!

I went down hard—and smacked my face in the dirt.

"OW!"

Shaking off the pain, I sat up.
"Oh, nooo," I moaned.
My glasses were broken.

**"AWWWWK! LUCKY LIPPY!
LUCKY LIPPY!"**

Chapter 7

GET OUT THE MOP

April-May stood over me. Her blond ponytail waved in the breeze. She gazed down with laughing blue eyes. "Ha-ha. Do that again!" she said.

"I did it on purpose," I said. "Just to give you a laugh. I always like to start the day with a laugh—don't you?"

She smiled. "Your face *always* makes me laugh, Bernie," she said.

"Thanks," I said. "That was a compliment, right?"

"For sure," she replied.

"Help me up," I said. I reached out my hand.

She stuck her chewing gum into my palm. Then

she took off, running to class.

That girl is just plain *crazy* about me.

Groaning, I pulled myself to my feet. I tucked my broken glasses into my shirt pocket. "That proves it," I told Lippy. "Your luck has run out."

"AWWWWK. YOU'RE A DUMB TWEET!"

I ignored the bird and staggered to the dorm. My buddies and I live in the dorm called Rotten House. It's actually a run-down old house on the edge of campus. And we love it.

Mrs. Heinie is our dorm mother. We all love Mrs. Heinie, mainly because she's very nearsighted. That means we can get away with pretty much anything!

This morning, Mrs. Heinie was in the Commons Room, our living room, picking up crinkled soda cans and empty tortilla chip bags guys had tossed around last night.

I crept in on tiptoe, heading for the stairs. I had to get to my room on the third floor without her seeing me. I knew I'd be in major trouble with Mrs. H. if she saw that I'd been out all night.

Softly … softly … I crept along the wall silently … holding my breath.

I nearly made it to the stairs when Lippy let out a loud,

"AWWWWK. BERNIE IS A SNEAK! BERNIE IS A SNEAK!"

Mrs. Heinie spun around and squinted at me through her thick eyeglasses. "Bernie? Sneaking in at eight in the morning?" she said.

"I can explain, Mrs. H.," I said. "I just joined the Wake Up at Dawn Club, and I—"

"AWWWK. ALL-NIGHT UNO. WHO LOVES IT? ALL-NIGHT UNO! WHO LOVES IT?"

Huh? I couldn't believe this! Now the bird was *snitching* on me?!

"He's joking," I told Mrs. Heinie. "The bird loves to joke."

"So do I," said Mrs. Heinie. "Bernie, do you know a good joke about scrubbing the kitchen floor?"

37

Uh-oh.

"No. I don't know that joke," I said.

She handed me a mop and a bucket. "Get started," she said. "Maybe you'll learn it."

"AWWWK. YOU'RE A DUMB TWEET!"

"Oh, really?" said Mrs. Heinie. "Well, then, you can scrub all the bathroom floors, too."

The bird did it to me again!

I felt like mopping the floor with Lippy! My big-mouthed parrot was *definitely* BAD LUCK.

As I mopped the floors, I asked myself the same questions over and over: What happened to Lucky Lippy? How can I get the good luck back?

"AWWWK. YOU MISSED A SPOT! YOU MISSED A SPOT!"

Chapter 8

Is There a Cure for Bad Luck?

When I finally finished mopping, my hands were red and swelled up like balloons. I was hot and sweaty and not feeling in tip-top shape.

I trudged up the stairs to my room on the third floor. My good buddy Belzer was waiting for me. He had a big tray in his hands. "I figured you'd be tired, Big B," he said. "So I brought you a small lunch from the Dining Hall."

Good kid, Belzer.

I lifted the lid off the tray. Belzer had brought two hamburgers, two plates of fries, a chili dog, a bowl of coleslaw, two pickles, two slices of pepperoni pizza, a bowl of tomato soup, a turkey club sandwich, a bowl of red and green grapes, and two thick shakes, one chocolate, one strawberry.

"Pretty light," I said. "But no problem. I'll grab a snack later."

"I put ketchup on each French fry," Belzer said. "And I tasted each grape to make sure they were all sweet."

"You're the man!" I said. I handed Lippy to him. "Put him into his cage and cover it with a heavy blanket. I never want to see him again."

"AWWWWK. MAKE ME PECK YOU TILL YOU BLEED!"

"Are you sure this is your parrot?" Belzer asked. "He looks like a bald eagle."

I sighed. "Feenman and Crench rubbed the feathers off his head. And I think they rubbed all the good luck off, too."

Belzer petted Lippy's bald head. Lippy bit his little finger off.

"The feathers will grow back," Belzer said when

he finally stopped screaming.

"I can't wait around for feathers to grow," I said. "Look how much bad luck he already brought me!" I waved my hand—and spilled the thick strawberry shake into my lap.

"See? *See?*" I cried. "And strawberry is my favorite! I can't *take* this!"

Belzer scrunched up his face till it looked like a closed fist. That's how you can tell when he's trying to think.

"Maybe Nurse Hanley knows a way to fix Lippy," he said.

"Yes!" I cried. I jumped up excitedly—and spilled the rest of the food all over my shoes. "Yes! Nurse Hanley!"

I grabbed the bird around the neck and started to the door. I knew Nurse Hanley could help. Nurse Hanley is a genius!

I mean, when Belzer woke up one morning and couldn't walk, we were all terrified. But it was Nurse Hanley who instantly saw that his shoes were on backward.

And two weeks ago, Feenman cut his knee trying

to walk on the ceiling. Nurse Hanley did a brilliant job of bandaging it. It turned out she bandaged the *wrong leg*. But it didn't matter. By the time she finished, the bleeding had stopped, anyway.

Brilliant!

Her office door was closed. I gave it four or five hard knocks. "Nurse Hanley? Are you in there?"

Then I saw a little handwritten sign next to the door. My glasses were broken. I had to squint to read it:

Sorry,
Will be away for a few days. If you are in pain, try screaming. Sometimes it helps.   Nurse Hanley

I couldn't believe it.
More bad luck for me.
I stared at the bald bird in my hands.
What should I do now?

Chapter 9

LIPPY TAKES
A POWDER

I walked across the Great Lawn, carrying Lippy back to the dorm. As I passed the statue of I. B. Rotten, I saw that spoiled rich kid Sherman Oaks. Why was he surrounded by a big bunch of kids?

As I walked closer, I saw that Sherman was showing off a new bike. "It has a 3-D navigation system," Sherman told the crowd. "I just pedal, and it steers itself."

"WOWWW."

A lot of kids were impressed.

"The bike has six cup holders," Sherman said. "Is that cool, or what?"

I tried to hurry away, but Sherman spotted me. "Hey, Bernie—another you-know-what tournament tonight?"

"Sorry. Can't do it," I said. "I promised Mrs. Heinie I'd help her with her knitting."

No way I could play cards with Sherman or anyone else. Not with Unlucky Lippy around. I'd lose big-time!

I trotted off, and a few steps later—*more* bad luck. I ran into Angel Goodeboy.

Angel is blond and blue-eyed and apple-cheeked and sweet looking. He looks like he should have a halo over his head.

With his sweet smile and good manners, Mrs. Heinie, Headmaster Upchuck, and all the grownups think he's a perfect angel.

But I know the truth about Angel. He's NOT an angel—unless you spell Angel like this: *R-A-T.*

"What's up, Angel?" I asked.

He flashed me his dazzling, angelic smile. "I'm so

excited, Bernie. My favorite cousin, Jolly Goodfellow, is coming to visit."

Angel's smile faded. He squinted at Lippy. "Oh, my gosh and golly!" he exclaimed. "What happened to your lovely bird?"

I shrugged. "No big deal. He lost a few feathers."

Angel patted my shoulder and smiled that blinding smile again. "Bernie, you're in luck. I can help repair Lippy."

My mouth dropped open. "Repair him? How?"

"My parents keep birds at home," Angel said. "They have twenty lovebirds. Oh, my gosh. Sometimes the cooing keeps me up all night."

"That's too bad," I said.

"All the Goodeboys love birds," Angel said. "My cousin Bigboy Goodeboy keeps parakeets in his pockets."

"Thanks for sharing that with me," I said.

"Anyway," Angel continued, "I have a very special jar of bird powder in my dorm room. I was going to bring it to my parents as a gift."

I stared at him. "Bird powder? What does it do?"

"Oh, my gosh and golly. It makes feathers grow

back instantly," Angel said. "I'll go get it for you, Bernie."

Angel trotted off toward his dorm. "I hate to see a bird with a bald spot," he said. "We don't want that poor thing to catch cold."

I stood there and watched him run all the way. "What an angel that dude is," I told myself. "Maybe I got him all wrong."

I carried Lippy back to my room. "In a few minutes, you're going to be beautiful," I said. "And you'll be my lucky bird again."

He plopped some green gunk onto my shirt.

"BITE A WALNUT, BIRD FACE!"

I laughed.

"AWWWWK. YOUR MOTHER EATS BIRDSEED!"

I set Lippy down onto his perch by the window. A few minutes later, Feenman and Crench shuffled in. Huge wads of pink bubble gum made their cheeks bulge.

Crench blew a big bubble and popped it with his

finger. The gum exploded over his face and stuck to his cheeks, his forehead, and his hair. It didn't seem to bother him. He just left it there.

Feenman handed me a small yellow jar. "Angel said to give this to you, Big B. What is it?"

I kissed the jar. "This is precious. Precious!" I said. "It's feather-growing powder. For Lippy."

Crench made a grab for the jar. "Better try some on Feenman first," he said. "You know. A test."

"You're already a *featherbrain!*" Feenman said.

"Give it a rest," I said. "This is serious. You want bad luck for the rest of your life? We've gotta fix this bird."

I walked over to Lippy and opened the jar. I rubbed some of the yellow powder onto my fingers.

Feenman and Crench grew silent. The only sound in the room was the snapping and popping of their bubble gum.

SNAP POP POP
POP SNAP POP
SNAP POP SNAP
POP

Carefully…

Carefully…I started to rub the powder onto Lippy's bald head.

Would it work?

Chapter 10

ANGEL'S LITTLE JOKE

"AAAAAAAAACHOOOOOO!"

A sneeze exploded from my mouth and nose.
Powder flew up from the jar in a yellow cloud.

"AAAAAAAACHOOOOOOOOEY!"

I sneezed again. A loud, wet, powerful sneeze.

"Oh, *no*!" I let out a cry as I realized I'd SNEEZED
so hard, I sneezed some of Lippy's feathers right off
him!

"AAAAACHOOOOO!"

"YAAAAAAACHOOOOOOEY!"
"ACHOOOOOOOOOOO!"

I sneezed again. Again.
Feenman sneezed.
Crench sneezed.
Feathers flew. Powder flew.
LIPPY sneezed!

"YAAAAAACHOOOEY!"
"AIIIIIIICHOOOOOOO!"

Belzer stumbled into the room. "Yo. What's up?"

"YA~YA~YACHHOOOOOO!"

Belzer sneezed so hard, his pants fell down. He reached for his pants—and sneezed again.

I sneezed some more. Sneezed so hard, I couldn't breathe.

Lippy sneezed. More feathers went flying.

I turned away from him—and saw someone standing in the doorway watching us.

Angel Goodeboy.

He raised his hands to his round, pink cheeks. His blue eyes went wide. "Oh, my gosh and golly," he said.

A grin spread over his angelic face. "Did I make a little mistake?" he asked. "Did I *accidentally* give you the jar of *sneezing powder* I got from a joke Web site?"

He pressed his hands to his cheeks. "Oh, my gosh and golly. My bad. My bad! How could I make such a horrid mistake?"

He turned and hurried away. I heard him laughing all the way down the stairs.

That proved it once and for all. Angel was no angel.

"YAAAAIIIICHOOOEY!"

I sneezed again—and watched the rest of Lippy's feathers go sailing into the air. I looked up. It was *raining feathers* in the room!

"Unnnh...unnnnh..." Feenman wiped the snot off his face with Crench's shirtsleeve. "Bernie—that bird...he's totally BALD!"

Crench picked up Lippy and used him as a hand-kerchief.

"Put him down," I muttered. "He's had a bad enough day, hasn't he? Why does he have to wipe your nose?"

I frowned at the limp, scrawny, naked bird and shook my head sadly. "You're bad luck," I said. "Bad-Luck Lippy. You have to go. Or else I'll never have good luck again."

Feenman and Crench both gasped. "He'll have to go? Do you mean it, Bernie?" Crench asked. "You're gonna get rid of him?"

I nodded. I had tears in my eyes. My stomach felt as tight as a knot. "We have no choice," I whispered. "My poor pet parrot—he has to go."

But ... where?

Chapter 11

GOOD NEWS, BAD NEWS

It broke my heart—but what choice did I have?

I waited till all the kids were on their way to dinner in the Dining Hall. I couldn't eat. I was too upset.

I put Lippy into his cage and carried it to the side of the girls' dorm. I set the cage down in the grass next to the door.

I blew Lippy a kiss. "Don't worry," I said. "A nice girl will adopt you and give you a good home."

"AWWWWK. BYE-BYE, BIRDBRAIN!"

56

He was so cute. I almost changed my mind.

But...no way. I had to leave my bad luck behind.

I blew him another kiss, forced myself to turn away—and ran all the way back to Rotten House.

"Bernie? Bernie—come here a minute." Mrs. Heinie stopped me at the stairs.

Uh-oh. Was this good luck or bad?

"Uh . . . sorry, Mrs. H.," I said. "No time to talk right now. I'm skipping dinner tonight. You know I like to study for at least six hours every night. Four hours just isn't enough. I want to learn, learn, learn!"

She rolled her eyes. "Tell me another one," she said. "Bernie, I *know* Belzer does your homework for you every night."

"No way," I said. "I do all the thinking. He just writes it down."

"Bernie, give me a break," Mrs. Heinie said. "I just want to congratulate you. You did such a *wonderful* mopping job. I think you deserve an extra dessert tonight!"

"*Yessss!*"

Lippy was gone for only two minutes—and my luck was changing already!

I thanked Mrs. Heinie and hurried to the Dining Hall. On the way, I found a crisp dollar bill lying in the grass. More good luck! And *two* desserts waiting for me!

Could life get any better?

Later that night, I even found my spare set of glasses. I sat in my room watching Belzer do my homework. I looked up when I heard a knock at the door.

"Yo, Bernie!" Angel Goodeboy walked in—carrying the birdcage with Lippy inside it.

Angel's blue eyes twinkled. "Bernie, I found your parrot by the girls' dorm," he said. "I rescued him for you. Please—don't thank me. I know how crazy you are about this bird!"

"But—but—" I sputtered.

Angel giggled. Then he set the cage down and hurried away.

Another knock on the door. Mrs. Heinie poked her head in. "By the way, Bernie," she said. "You did such a great cleaning job, I want you to mop the floors *every week!*"

I let out a long groan. Bad luck. Bad luck for Bernie B.

Bad-Luck Lippy was back.

Chapter 12

BERNIE THE HUMAN PRETZEL

The next morning, I heard thundering hoofbeats again as I headed across the Great Lawn to class. I tried to run, but Jennifer Ecch tackled me from behind and dropped me to the ground.

"Good morning, Sweet Cakes," she said. She sat on my chest so I couldn't escape.

"Don't call me Sweet Cakes," I said, spitting grass from between my teeth. "What do you want, Jennifer?"

She took my hand and licked it for a while. I told you—she's crazy nuts about me.

"Jennifer, please—I just had a shower," I said.

"Remember about the I. B. Rotten Games?" she asked. "You and I are going to be a great team—aren't we, Bernie Face?"

"Uh . . . I can't breathe," I gasped. "I think you crushed my ribs to sawdust."

She giggled. "You know I want to win every game and take home the I. B. Rotten Trophy."

"T-trophy?" I stammered, feeling my lungs collapse beneath her.

"I collect trophies," The Ecch said. "I have two thousand of them in my dorm room. Just the ones I could bring from home."

"N-nice," I choked out.

She leaned over me and narrowed her brown eye and her blue eye to slits. "You'd better not mess up, Goo-Goo Eyes," she said. "You'd better help me win every game. I'd *hate* to do some more arm cracking! I'd hate to bend you into a pretzel."

Yikes! *More arm cracking? Pretzel bending?*

I *need* my arms to play Uno!

"Hey, I'm a winner," I said. "No way we can lose!"

She climbed off, lifted me up with one hand, and

dusted me off with the other. Then she gave my hand one last, long, sticky lick with her big cow tongue and thundered off to class.

No way we can *win*, I thought sadly. Not with Bad-Luck Lippy around.

The Ecch will be cracking my arms into talcum powder.

Unless...

Suddenly, I knew what I had to do.

I ran back to the dorm and picked up Lippy in his cage. I carried the cage to the middle of R.U. Dumm Field, our soccer field.

I pulled open the cage door and lifted my sweet parrot out. Then I held him in both hands in front of me.

I had tears in my eyes. My whole body was trembling. But I had no choice.

I raised Lippy high—and tossed him into the sky.

"You're free, Lippy!" I cried. "Free! Fly away! Fly away, free!"

Chapter 13

"WHAT HAVE I DONE?"

Tears blurred my eyes. But I watched Lippy flap his wings and fly. He sailed up to the clouds, turned, and flew away.

I brushed away my tears. "He'll have a happier life," I told myself. "And so will I."

I trudged to class, thinking about my sweet bird and all his clever, adorable sayings. I didn't hear a word Mrs. Heinie said all morning.

At lunch in the Dining Hall, my stomach was doing somersaults. I couldn't eat a thing.

My friend Beast dipped his head into my plate

and gobbled down my entire lunch. Beast does that to everyone. That's why he usually sits alone.

I didn't care about food. I was too upset over my tragic loss.

When I got outside, I realized Beast had also eaten my *shirt*!

Mrs. Heinie wouldn't let me back into class with a bare chest. So I made my way back to Rotten House.

All across the Great Lawn, kids were laughing, singing, dancing, pushing each other into Pooper's Pond. I wished I could be happy, too.

But I just kept muttering to myself, "What have I done? What have I *done?*"

I pulled myself up the stairs to the third floor and stepped into my room.

And there sat Lippy on his perch by the open window.

"AWWWWK! BITE MY TOENAILS!"

Chapter 14

WHO DESERVES A LITTLE BAD LUCK?

"Lippy! You're home!" I cried happily.

I ran across the room with outstretched arms. "Here's a big hug! Here's a big hug for my pretty bird!"

Halfway to the window, I tripped over some books on the floor, fell hard—and cut both knees.

Bad Luck Lippy strikes again.

Forget the hug. The bird had to go!

I bandaged my knees. Then I picked up the squawking bad-luck bird and carried him outside.

The Bernie B. brain was plugging and chugging.

I knew Lippy wouldn't *fly* away. But maybe…maybe I could *give* him away!

I walked past the girls' dorm. No one around. I turned and crossed R.U. Dumm Field. Some third graders had an air soccer game going.

Can you imagine playing soccer without a ball?! *No way* I'd trust any of them with my precious Lippy!

I followed the path across the Great Lawn. I heard a growl and saw Beast down on all fours, chasing a squirrel. Maybe Beast would like a pet, I thought.

But no. Bad idea. Beast ate a *chipmunk* last week on a dare.

"Who needs a nice parrot?" I asked myself. "Who deserves a little bad luck?"

And then I saw Sherman Oaks. He was standing in the middle of a crowd of kids. Sherman, my old buddy. What do you give a kid who already has *everything*?

A bad-luck parrot, of course.

Sherman was showing off, as usual. The kids were all oohing and aahing as Sherman demonstrated his new, solid gold cell phone.

"The screen lights up, and the back lights up, and the *sides* light up," Sherman said. "When you hold it, your *hand* lights up!"

"OOOOH!"

"AAAAAH!"

"This phone is so powerful," Sherman said, "it picks up calls *from other planets!*"

"OOOOOH!"

"AAAAAAH!"

Sherman is the luckiest dude on earth, I decided. Should I give Lippy to him and change his luck?

How *great* would that be?

The idea got me so excited, I squeezed Lippy a little too hard.

He made a gagging sound and spit up some yellow

gunk onto my school blazer.

"Yo! Sherman!" I shouted. I pushed my way through the crowd. "Sherman, I've got something special for you, dude! This is your lucky day!"

Chapter 15

BIRD PLOP FOR BRAINS

Sherman wasn't finished showing off his phone. "With this phone, I can call people I don't even know!" he said.

"AAAAAH!"
"OOOOOH!"

His phone rang. Sherman let out a cry of surprise. He raised the phone to his ear. "Hello? Who is this?"

"It's me," I said, speaking into my cell phone.

72

"I'm trying to get your attention."

Sherman lowered his phone and came walking over to me. "What do you want, Bernie?" He slipped the solid gold phone into his shirt.

"It's your lucky day," I said. "I decided to sell this rare, Patagonian parrot."

"AWWWWK! WHERE WERE YOU HATCHED?"

Sherman stared at Lippy. "Where are his feathers? He's totally bald!"

"That's what makes him rare," I said. "I know you want to pay two hundred dollars for him. But you're my old pal, Shermie. I'll sell him to you for ten bucks."

"No thanks," Sherman said.

"Okay, okay," I said. "Three dollars. And I'll throw in his perch. That's my final price."

"No thanks," Sherman said.

"Okay," I said. "You drive a hard bargain. You can have him for free. Go ahead. Take him. Tell you what—I'll pay *you* five dollars."

"No thanks," Sherman said.

This was tough. Sherman wasn't buying. But I knew I had to keep trying.

Bernie B. is always an honest guy. Except when a little white lie might help smooth things out. Like maybe now.

"I'll tell you the truth," I said. "The total truth. Lippy is a good-luck charm."

Sherman's eyes grew wide. He squinted at Lippy. "He *is?*"

"If you have Lippy on your shoulder, you can't lose," I said. "Sherman, why do you think I win every Uno game?"

"Because you cheat?"

"No. Because I always have Lippy with me."

"AWWWWK. BIRD PLOP FOR BRAINS!"

Sherman reached out and fingered Lippy's bald head. "He's really lucky?" he asked.

I finally had him hooked.

"If you take the parrot, I'll never beat you at Uno again," I said. "You'll win every game. You'll never lose at *anything.* You'll see."

He petted Lippy's head again. "Anything?"

"AWWWK."

Lippy snapped his beak and bit part of Sherman's thumb off.

"That's *lucky!*" I said. "If he bites you like that, it means you'll have good luck for a week."

"Okay. I'll take him," Sherman said. "You sure he's a good-luck charm?"

I perched Lippy on Sherman's shoulder. The bird dug his claws through Sherman's shirt.

"That's even *more* good luck!" I said.

Sherman turned and walked off smiling, with Lippy squawking on his shoulder.

"More good luck for ME!" I said softly.

With that bad-luck bird gone, I could feel the *good* luck flowing back to me.

I pumped my fists into the air. I did a little celebration dance.

Across the lawn, Sherman tripped over a garden hose and fell flat on his perfectly tanned face.

Chapter 16

TIME TO START ACKING

Saturday afternoon in the Student Center, I planned to study with Feenman and Crench. Don't get the wrong idea. It's not like we do schoolwork on a Saturday afternoon. We were going to study some new bubble gum flavors.

You know. Serious stuff.

I wandered into the game room and saw Sherman at the Ping-Pong table. Sharonda Davis, April-May's friend, was at the other end. Sharonda and Sherman were slamming the ball back and forth over the net at each other. They were grunting and sweating and running from side to side.

"No way Sherman can win," I told myself. He had Bad-Luck Lippy on his shoulder. That meant he couldn't win at Ping-Pong if he used a tennis racket for a paddle!

"AWWWWK.
LICK MY PERCH!
LICK MY PERCH!"

I watched the battle for a while. They both worked up a sweat. Sharonda slammed the ball so hard, it cracked and flew off the table.

Finally, she threw down her paddle, muttering to herself. "I don't believe it....I don't believe you beat me again, Sherman."

Sherman came over to me, a big sixty-five-tooth smile on his face. "Thanks, Bernie," he said. "You were right about Lippy."

"Excuse me?" My mouth dropped open. "What do you mean?"

"I won twelve straight games," Sherman said. He petted Lippy's bald head. "Thanks to my lucky parrot."

"AWWWWWK.
I'LL PECK YOUR EAR WAX!"

Weird. Sharonda is a champion Ping-Pong player.

"Gotta hurry," Sherman said. He pulled out a leopard-skin handkerchief and wiped the sweat off his forehead. "I'm meeting April-May."

Huh? He was meeting MY girlfriend?

"We're going to have a picnic at Pooper's Pond," Sherman said.

"Aaack, aaack aaack,"

I said. I was too choked up to talk.

I followed him out of the Student Center. April-May was waiting for him. Her blue eyes flashed, and she gave him a big smile.

She wrapped her arm in his. "Shermie, you're so cute with that adorable parrot on your shoulder," she gushed.

Shermie?? Adorable parrot??

"Aaack, aaack aaack,"

I couldn't stop *ack*ing.

Arm in arm, they started to walk away. Suddenly, Sherman stopped. He bent down and picked something up from the grass.

"Check it out, April-May," he said. "I just found a twenty-dollar bill!"

"Aaack!"

Sherman? Suddenly lucky?

"Calm down, Big B. This can't be happening," I told myself. "Wait till the all-night Uno tournament tonight. We'll *see* who's lucky!"

Chapter 17

"URRRRRRP," CRENCH REPLIED

Sherman won every game that night. He took every dime I had.

And the whole night, that stupid parrot on his shoulder kept squawking:

"LUCKY LIPPY! LUCKY LIPPY!"

Finally, I handed my wallet to Sherman. "Keep it," I said. "I don't have anything left to put into it."

"Thanks, Bernie," Sherman replied, slapping me on the back. "I couldn't have done it without you!" Then he laughed for about ten minutes.

What a sore winner!

I staggered back to the dorm. I could still hear that parrot squawking and crowing.

I trudged into Feenman and Crench's room and dropped weakly onto the edge of their bunk bed. "Root beer," I moaned. "Bring me gallons of Foamy Root Beer. I love Foamy Root Beer."

Feenman pulled some cans out from their hiding place under his mountain of dirty clothes. The three of us drank silently for a while, wiping the foam off our faces with the backs of our hands.

After a three- or four-minute burping session, I shook my head sadly. "Thanks to that traitor parrot," I moaned, "Sherman is now the luckiest dude in school."

"Who knew the bird would turn lucky again?" Feenman said.

"URRRRRRP."

Crench wasn't finished burping.

Foamy Root Beer is very bubbly. Sometimes after you drink it, you burp for two or three days.

"Sherman is bragging all over campus," Feenman

said. "He says he's going to win *every game* at the I. B. Rotten Competition."

"He *is* going to win every game," Crench said. "With Lucky Lippy, no way he can lose."

I slapped my forehead. "What am I going to do?" I moaned. "When are those games? The day after tomorrow, right?"

"URRRRRRP."

Crench replied.

"Jennifer says she and I have to win every game," I said, shuddering. "If I don't get that bird back, she'll...she'll..."

I knew exactly what Jennifer would do to me. Crack my arms and bend me into a pretzel.

But I couldn't say it. "*Aaaack, aaaack.*" I started *ack*ing again.

"Get Bernie some more soda," Crench said.

Feenman dove under his dirty clothes pile.

"*Aaaaack.* No time for root beer," I moaned. "I've got to get Lippy back from Sherman. Now."

Chapter 18

GASSY SHOWS OFF

The next day, I brought my pet bulldog, Gassy, over to Nyce House, Sherman's dorm. You can probably guess how my dog got his name.

I found Sherman in the Commons Room with Wes Updood and a bunch of his buddies. He had Lippy on his shoulder. And believe it or not, Sherman was still showing off his new gold cell phone.

"See this bright yellow light? Know what that's for?" Sherman asked. "It's so I can tell which pants pocket the phone is in!"

"OOOOH!"
"AAAAAAH!"

"It's like a cherry in your ear," Wes Updood said to me. "Without the stem. Know what I'm saying?"

"No," I said.

Gassy wagged his stub of a tail.

"Wet dogs don't chew their food," Wes said. "But you can look up *fiduciary* if you don't know how to spell it. Know what I mean?"

"No," I said.

Wes is so awesomely cool, I wish I could understand him.

I pushed through the crowd and stepped up to Sherman. "I've gotta apologize," I said. "I did a bad thing."

Sherman slipped the cell phone into his pants pocket. I could see it glowing in there.

"I didn't give you the REAL lucky pet," I said. "And I feel bad about it, Sherm, because you're my buddy."

I pushed my sweet bulldog up to Sherman. "Here he is—the *real* good-luck guy. He'll bring you so much good luck, you won't know what hit you!"

Sherman squinted down at Gassy. "That *fat thing* is good luck?"

I nodded. "I feel so bad, here's what I'll do. I'll give you Gassy and take Lippy off your hands. It means I'm gonna have a lot of bad luck. But that's okay. I want to do the right thing."

I reached for Lippy.

But at that moment, Gassy decided to live up to his name.

We all heard it. And then we all smelled it.

It was BAD....So bad, it set off the smoke alarms!

Sherman's friends were gagging and retching and sick on the floor.

"Take Gassy, Sherman. Don't let his little stomach problems keep you from having good luck," I said.

Sherman dropped to his knees, holding his nose. "OUT!" he screamed. "OUT! I'm dying! I'm DYING!

Get that dog OUTTA here!"

BRRRAAAAAAAP!

"Okay, okay, don't shove," I said. "You don't want
good luck? Fine. I'm going."

Chapter 19

WHO'S A GOOD BIRD?

I'm a good guy. I'm not a thief.

But what choice did I have? Spend the rest of my life as a pretzel? Or steal Lippy away from Sherman?

That night, I paced back and forth in my room. Feenman popped his head in. "What's up, Bernie?

"What's up? What's up? How can you ask what's up?" I cried. "The games are tomorrow morning. You know I have to help my partner, The Ecch, win every game. What can I do?"

Feenman scratched his head. "I saw a movie about a boy who runs away from home and joins a circus.

He gets a job shoveling up after the elephants, and—"

"Stop right there," I said. "I'm allergic to big animals."

Feenman shrugged. "That's all I can think of."

"Thanks for your help," I said.

I already knew what I had to do. Sneak into Sherman's room and *steal* Lucky Lippy back.

A piece of cake. Sherman's room was in the back of Nyce House, on the first floor. All I had to do was climb in his window, grab the bird, and run.

I waited until midnight. Everyone was asleep. I crept down the stairs silently in my stocking feet. Then I pulled on my sneakers and slipped out the front door.

A cool, clear night. A full moon and hundreds of twinkling stars to lead my way across the silent, empty campus.

My heart pounded. Not from being scared. From happiness. Soon, all the good luck would be *mine* again—and just in time for the games!

I made my way around to the back of the dorm. Hunching low behind a row of bushes, I counted the windows to Sherman's room.

The window was open. I grabbed the window ledge and hoisted myself up. I peered inside to make sure I had the right room.

Yes. I could see Sherman's favorite poster on the wall—a poster of a big dollar sign.

I heaved myself onto the ledge and dropped silently into the room. I took a deep breath and held it, waiting for my eyes to adjust.

In the yellow moonlight coming through the window, I saw Sherman in his bed, wearing his favorite dollar-sign eye mask. He was sound asleep on his satin pillow, under his zebra-skin blanket.

I tiptoed around Sherman's bed. Lippy stood on his perch. His feathers had grown back. He was sound asleep, too. Perfect.

I carefully lifted the sleeping bird off the perch.

Holding Lippy in both hands, I turned and crept back to the window. The floorboards creaked under my feet. But Sherman didn't stir.

Holding the bird gently, I made it to the window. And started to lower myself outside.

That's when Lippy woke up. He lifted his head,

opened his beak, and squawked at the top of his lungs:

"SHERMAN IS A GOOD BIRD! SHERMAN IS A GOOD BIRD!"

Sherman's eyes bugged open, and he sat straight up with a startled cry. "Bernie! What are you *doing* in here?"

"I ... well ..." The Bernie B. brain began to whir. "I ... uh ..."

"What are you doing with *my parrot?*" Sherman cried.

"I . . . brought Lippy a midnight snack," I said. "You know. For old time's sake. His favorite prunes. He always loves some pitted prunes at midnight."

"OUT, Bernie!" Sherman yelled. "And leave my lucky bird alone!"

"No problem," I said. I set Lippy down. Then I jumped out the window and took off.

Behind me, I could hear Lippy squawking away:

"SHERMAN IS A GOOD BIRD!

SHERMAN IS A GOOD BIRD!"

I ran all the way back to my room. Then I picked up a salt shaker and began pouring salt all over myself. Might as well get a head start. I *knew* I'd be a pretzel by tomorrow afternoon!

Chapter 20

FEATHERS FLY

"Horseback riding is the first competition," Jennifer Ecch said. "You're a champion rider, aren't you, Bernie Babykins?"

"For sure," I said. "That horse is awfully tall, isn't it? Which end do I ride?"

Jennifer laughed and gave me a slap on the back that sent me stumbling into the horse's huge butt. "I love your jokes, Honey Chin. Saddle up. Let's win that trophy."

"No problem, Jen. Do you have a ladder or something I could use?"

She gave me another hard slap that sent me sprawling into the dirt. Ha-ha. Big joke, right?

There we were at Lake Choking Gas. The lake shimmered like gold in the morning sun. Pine trees dropped their needles onto the sandy shore. It was beautiful—if you held your nose.

They don't call it Lake Choking Gas for *nothing*!

The list of games had been posted on a tree by Coach Manley Bunz:

1. HORSEBACK RIDING
2. ARCHERY
3. ROWING
4. HORSESHOES
5. VOLLEYBALL
6. BENDING BERNIE INTO A PRETZEL

I know. That last one wasn't really on the list. But I knew Jennifer Ecch would probably be adding it soon.

I turned and watched Sherman and his partner, April-May. They walked their horses out onto the path. They were both petting Lippy for luck.

They had big grins on their faces. They knew they couldn't lose.

Coach Bunz walked over to them, his big belly bouncing in front of him. Coach's stomach always arrives five or ten seconds before he does.

My mouth dropped open. Coach Bunz was pointing to the silver I. B. Rotten Trophy. And he was already congratulating Sherman and April-May!

"This isn't happening," I muttered, shaking my head. "This can't happen to Bernie B."

Suddenly, I had an idea.

I saw Feenman and Crench down the path. They were partners. But I saw that they were off to a bad start. They had strapped the saddles onto their horses' stomachs, not their backs.

I called them over. Should I tell them their mistake?

"Dudes, do me favor," I said. "Remember when you rubbed all the good luck off Lippy?"

"It was an accident, Bernie," Feenman said. "We didn't mean to do it."

"Don't worry about it," I said. "Just go over to Sherman and do it again."

They stared at me. "Rub Lippy's feathers off again?" Crench said.

I nodded. "Beg Sherman to let you touch Lippy for luck. Then rub him bald again."

"No problem," Feenman said. "Maybe it'll give Crench and me good luck, and *we'll* win the Rotten Trophy."

I looked at their horses. Saddles on their stomachs. Pitiful.

"Yeah. Maybe you dudes will get lucky," I said.

And maybe I'll lay an egg at breakfast tomorrow.

Feenman and Crench turned and trotted down the bridle path to Sherman and April-May. I watched them beg and plead with Sherman to let them touch Lippy.

Then I watched them pick the bird up— and rub Lippy like crazy.

Feathers flew.
Lippy was bald
again. I could see
the goose bumps on his yellow skin.

"Good work, dudes!" I shouted.

But would it work?

Would it turn Lippy into a bad-luck bird again?

Would it turn Sherman into the big loser of the day?

Chapter 21

L-O-S-E-R

The answer to those questions is a very big YES!

Bad-Luck Lippy instantly became WORST LUCK Lippy!

With the parrot on his shoulder, poor Sherman didn't stand a chance. He should have tattooed *L-O-S-E-R* on his forehead!

I would *never* call myself a *genius*, of course. I'll leave that to you. But here's how it went down:

HORSEBACK RIDING: Jennifer and I won easily after Lippy scared Sherman's horse and it ran headfirst into a tree. The horse staggered around like it was drunk, and Sherman had to hitch a ride with April-May.

ARCHERY: Sherman was about to let his arrow go at the target. Lippy let out a deafening squawk. Sherman's arm jumped. And he shot his arrow into Coach Bunz's butt. Bernie and Jennifer win again.

ROWING: Just as Sherman and April-May were nearing the finish line, Worst Luck Lippy fell out of the boat. Sherman dove into the lake to save him. April-May had to drag them both out of Lake Choking Gas—stinking to high heaven. By that time, Jennifer and Bernie B. had won the race.

HORSESHOES: Sherman and April-May were winning—until Worst Luck Lippy dug his claws into Sherman's shoulder. Sherman clonked *himself* in the head with a horseshoe and had to go lie down under a tree. Another big victory for Bernie and The Ecch.

VOLLEYBALL: Sherman got his head stuck in the net. Yes, the bad-luck parrot struck again. It took Nurse Hanley an hour to untangle it. Sherman had net marks all over his face! Bernie and Jen won again, just to make it a perfect day.

"YAAAAAAY!" Jennifer went totally nuts.

She lifted me off the ground and ran around the lake, holding me over her head like a prize fish and cheering her head off. "We won! We won the trophy!"

The Ecch really loves trophies.

She made three laps around the lake, tossing me into the air and catching me as she ran. Then everyone gathered in a circle around Coach Bunz. It was time for Coach to award the trophy.

Snarling like a dog, Sherman stormed up to me. He shoved Lippy into my face. "Take this squawker back!" Sherman shouted. "He's yours. He's totally bad luck. He even broke my new phone!"

"Yessss!" I cried. I pumped my fists into the air. Then I gently placed Lippy on my shoulder.

I had my beautiful pet back. And I helped Jennifer win her precious trophy.

Could life be any sweeter?

How long would the good times last?

About thirty seconds.

Chapter 22

FLAT BERNIE

"The Rotten Trophy is not about *winning*," Coach Bunz boomed. "And it's not about *losing*. It's all about *tradition*. The tradition of ... of winning and losing."

He took a deep breath. His stomach inflated like a blimp. He continued his speech. "On this beautiful morning—or is it afternoon? Let me check my watch. It's ..."

"Just hand over the trophy!" Jennifer snapped.

"Oh. Okay," Coach Bunz said. He picked up the gleaming silver cup and handed it to me.

I turned and started to carry it over to Jennifer.

107

That's when Lippy climbed onto my head. I felt something warm and gloppy plop onto my forehead. It oozed down over my eyes and …

…I *tripped*!

I stumbled and fell.

And guess where I landed. You got it. *On the trophy*.

I heard a loud

CRUNNNCH.

At first, I thought it was my *bones*!

But no. Wiping bird glop off my face, I pulled myself up. And squinted down at the trophy beneath me.

Flat. I'd crushed it flat.

I turned and saw The Ecch shaking her big fist at me. "You RUINED it! You RUINED my trophy!"

I took off running. Running for my life.

"Stop! STOP, you trophy wrecker!" Jennifer screamed. She thundered after me, shaking her big fist like a club. "How does the name Flat Bernie sound to you?"

Not good.

I ran as hard as I could. And as I ran, the bad-news parrot squawked all the way:

"LUCKY LIPPY! AWWWK!
LUCKY LIPPY! LUCKY LIPPY!"

HERE'S A SNEAK PEEK AT BOOK #16

R.L. STINE'S

ROTTEN SCHOOL

DUMB CLUCKS

A Birdbrain that Thinks

BLUCK. BLUCK. BLUCK.
BLUCK. BLUCK. BLUCK. BLUCK. BLUCK.
BLUCK. BLUCK. BLUCK. BLUCK.

All my friends were *blucking*.

"Why are you *blucking*?" I asked. "Are you watching a TV show called BLUCK?"

Everyone groaned.

"We're watching *Stupid Chicken*, Bernie," Feenman said.

"He's totally awesome," Crench said. "He has Drumsticks of Doom!"

"And Buffalo Wings of Steel," Belzer added.

I turned to Chipmunk. He's the shyest kid in school. He had a blindfold pulled down over his eyes. Chipmunk only *listens* to TV. He's too shy to watch it.

"Chipmunk, *you're* loyal to the Tadpoles—aren't you?" I asked. "Isn't *that* your favorite TV show?"

Chipmunk cleared his throat for about ten minutes. It's one of his most disturbing habits. "The Tadpoles are kinda violent," he whispered. He started to tremble.

"Bernie, don't you watch *Stupid Chicken?*" Belzer asked. "It's the most popular cartoon on *Chickelodeon.*"

"It comes on every night after *Teriyaki Chicken,*" Feenman said. "You know. The Karate Klucker?"

"Huh?" I stared at the TV screen. There was Stupid Chicken. A fat yellow chicken in a blue-and-red cape. He flew across the sky, blucking his head off.

"I don't believe you dudes are sitting here watching a flying chicken," I said. "How *could* you abandon the Tadpoles?"

The chicken flew into some kind of house made

3

of ice. "Who lives there?" I asked. "Frozen Chicken?"

The guys usually love my jokes. But nobody even smiled.

"That's the Henhouse of Solitude," Crench said. "That's where Stupid Chicken goes to think things over."

I rolled my eyes. "Oh, perfect. A birdbrain that *thinks*!"

I stared at the screen. "What's that dumb-looking featherball rolling behind Stupid Chicken?" I asked. "Something he coughed up after breakfast?"

Beast jumped to his feet and shook a fist at me. His fist was bigger than my head! "Are you making fun of America's National Chicken?" he boomed.

"Of course not," I said. I took several steps back. Beast can be dangerous. Especially if he hasn't had his rabies shots.

"That little featherball is Little Cluck-Cluck," Feenman said. "He's always getting into trouble. He's so funny."

I stared at my worthless pile of Tadpoles T-shirts. "Ha-ha," I said bitterly.

What was I gonna do with these shirts? No one

wanted to buy them.

Maybe I could take a marker and draw feathers on the Tadpoles. I'd tell the guys it's what Stupid Chicken looked like when he was a baby.

No. No way they'd believe it.

"Crench, tell me," I said. "How can a chicken be a superhero?"

"Are you kidding?" Crench said. "First he pecks your knees to bring you down. Then he kicks gravel on you."

"Exciting," I muttered.

I slapped the pile of T-shirts. I *had* to sell them to *somebody*!

Suddenly, I had an idea....

photo by Dan Nelken

R.L. Stine graduated from Rotten School with a solid D+ average, which put him at the top of his class. He says that his favorite activities at school were Scratching Body Parts and Making Armpit Noises.

In sixth grade, R.L. won the school Athletic Award for his performance in the Wedgie Championships. Unfortunately, after the tournament, his underpants had to be surgically removed.

R.L. was very popular in school. He could tell this because kids always clapped and cheered whenever he left the room. One of his teachers remembers him fondly: "R.L. was a hard worker. He was so proud of himself when he learned to wave bye-bye with both hands."

After graduation, R.L. became well known for writing scary book series such as The Nightmare Room, Fear Street, Goosebumps, and Mostly Ghostly, and a short story collection called *Beware!*

Today, R.L. lives in a cage in New York City, where he is busy writing stories about his school days. Says he: "I wish everyone could be a Rotten Student."

For more information
about R.L. Stine,
go to www.rottenschool.com
and www.rlstine.com